Ruthie Bon Bair

Do Not Go to Bed with Wringing Wet Hair!

by Susan Lubner

illustrated by Bruce Whatley

ABRAMS BOOKS FOR YOUNG READERS
NEW YORK

Designer: Vivian Cheng
Production Manager: Alexis Mentor

Library of Congress Cataloging-in-Publication Data:
Lubner, Susan.
Ruthie Bon Bair, do not go to bed with wringing wet hair! / by Susan Lubner.
p. cm.
Summary: After ignoring her mother's warnings, a young girl goes to
bed with wet hair and wakes up with a surprise on her head.
[1. Hair–Care and hygiene–Fiction. 2. Humorous stories. 3. Stories
in rhyme.] I. Title.

PZ8.3.L9559Ru 2006
[E]–dc22
2005011777

Printed and bound in Singapore
10 9 8 7 6 5 4 3 2 1

HNA ▊▊▊▊
harry n. abrams, inc.
a subsidiary of La Martinière Groupe
115 West 18th Street
New York, NY 10011
www.hnabooks.com

To my mother, Barbara, for all her wonderful advice.
And to anyone who has ever had a bad hair day . . . this is for you.
—S.L.

To Sara, Andy, and any future little Saras and Andys.
—B.W.

In the middle of winter, in a tucked away town,
Where the snow never seemed to stop coming down,
In a mountain-sized house the color of sky,
Lived a girl with thick hair that took too long to dry.
Her mother would plead, "Ruthie Bon Bair!
When you finish your bath, please dry you hair!"
But her hair often tangled, especially when wet.
Brushing and drying just made her upset.
Ruthie preferred to leave it alone,
And let her thick hair dry out on its own.

Something happened one morning that caused her to frown:
A grove of white mushrooms sprung up from her crown!
"What is this?" she screeched, so full of dismay.
"How did my head ever end up this way?"
"I've told you once and I've told you twice,"
Reminded her mother in a voice not so nice,
"Do not go to bed with a wringing wet head!
Use a brush, a comb, and a dryer instead.
Now try not to pout, I'll pull them all out."

But later that morning the mushrooms grew back.
And along with the white, there were yellow and black.
What Ruthie saw next sure gave her a start:
A tall trail of ferns poked right through her part!

And on the back of her noggin, so increasingly fertile,
Grew a mound of green moss in the shape of a turtle.

"It looks like a forest is growing up there!
Do something quick! Please save my hair!"
"I've told you once and I've told you twice,"
Reminded her mother in a voice not so nice,
"Do not go to bed with a wringing wet head!
Use a brush, a comb, and a dryer instead.
Now wipe off your tears, and I'll get my shears."

All through the next day, Ruthie's head was still troubled.

The mushrooms were back but their quantity doubled.

The feathery ferns, they, too, reappeared.

Not just in her part, but behind her left ear.

Ruthie peeked in the mirror and let out a yelp.

Six water lilies now clung to her scalp!

The house was soon crowded in all sorts of places
With lily-filled urns and overstuffed vases.
Decorative wreaths that were braided with blooms
Hung over each doorway of all eighteen rooms.
And served with each meal every day after day,
Was a fresh mushroom stew, a new soup, or soufflé.
"I've told you once and I've told you twice,"
Reminded her mother in a voice not so nice,
"Just look at the trouble your wet hair can bring.
I think we must now give the doctor a ring."

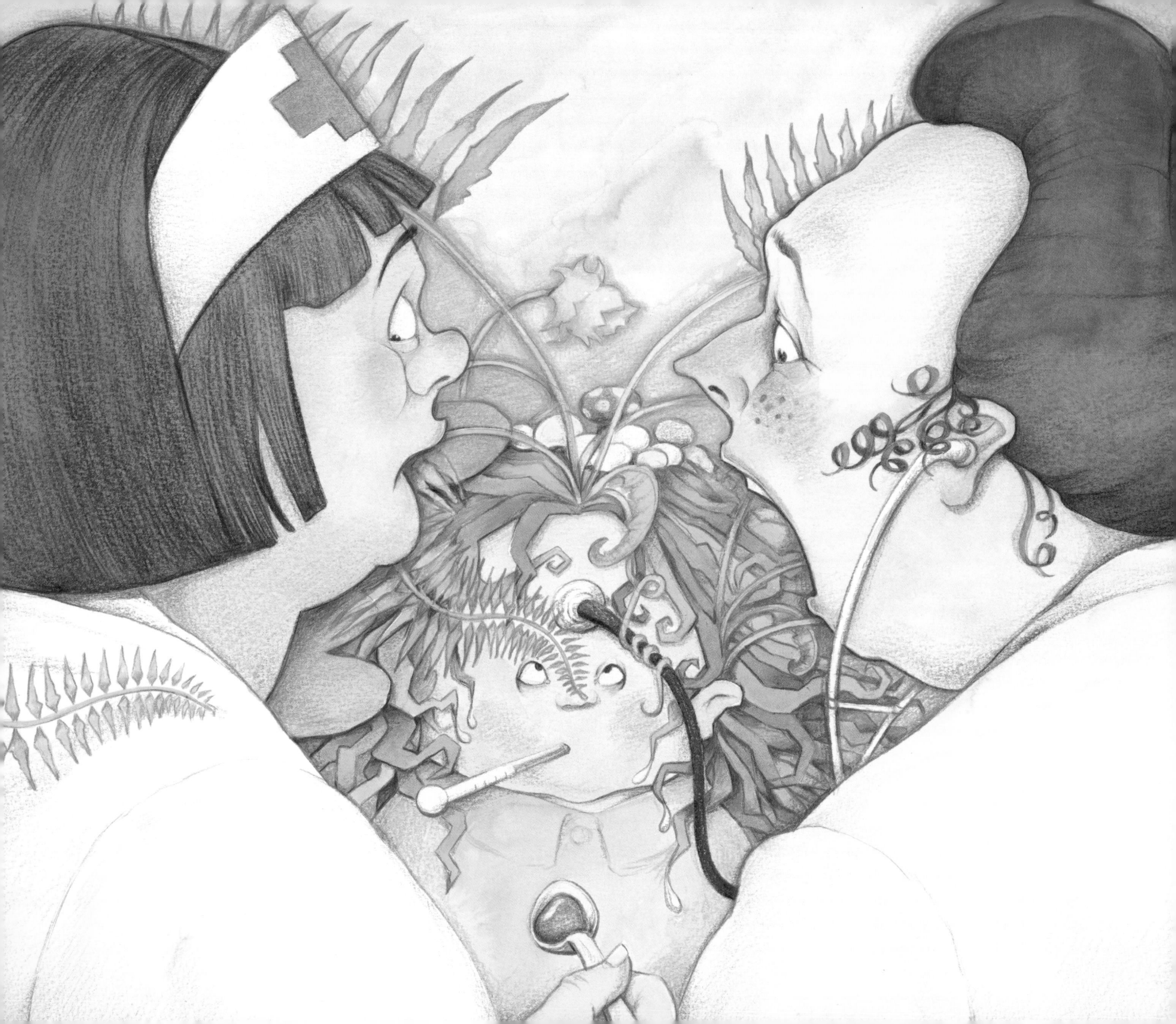

She came with her ointments, her potions, and nurse,
But the doctor seemed only to make matters worse.
She pinched, she poked, she pricked, and she prodded,
Then scratched at her head while the nurse simply nodded.
"I'm not able to help but I do have a plan:
Maybe the gardener could lend you a hand?"

The gardener had long ago packed up his hoe,
His pots, and his seeds at the first sign of snow.
It was all stored away until spring in his shed.
Then he said with regret while he studied her head,
"In all my experience with planting and sowing
I only know how to get plants to keep growing!
It seems Ruthie's roots do in fact need repair.
Perhaps you'll consider an expert in hair?"

The hairdresser came with his boxes and trays,
Filled with hair products—gels, tonics, and sprays.
He trimmed back the lilies and combed through the moss.
He pinned down the ferns and massaged in a gloss.
Then he sprayed and he teased, he ironed and creamed,
But the moss just looked thicker and the
   mushrooms now gleamed.
The hairdresser confessed, hands covered in goo,
"I've never seen anything quite like this 'do."

With the doctor, the nurse, and the hairdresser, too,

Ruthie's mom and the gardener discussed what to do.

A smile crossed the face of Ruthie Bon Bair,

For the weather outside had captured her stare.

With no coat and no boots, she ran out in the cold.

Then before her mother or others could scold,

She turned to them all and began to explain,

"Surely you all must think I am insane.

But the reason I'm out here like this in the snow

Is because in the winter, plants no longer grow!"

And just when the crowd had thought they'd seen the worst,

She dove into the snow and landed headfirst!

Her mom and the doctor tugged with their might.

The gardener and hairdresser pulled her upright.

The nurse wrapped her shoulders in a long woolly coat

And fastened a muffler around Ruthie's throat.

Covered in snow from her crown to her chin,

With dripping wet hair and goose-pimpled skin,

Ruthie shivered, she jittered, she shuddered and . . .

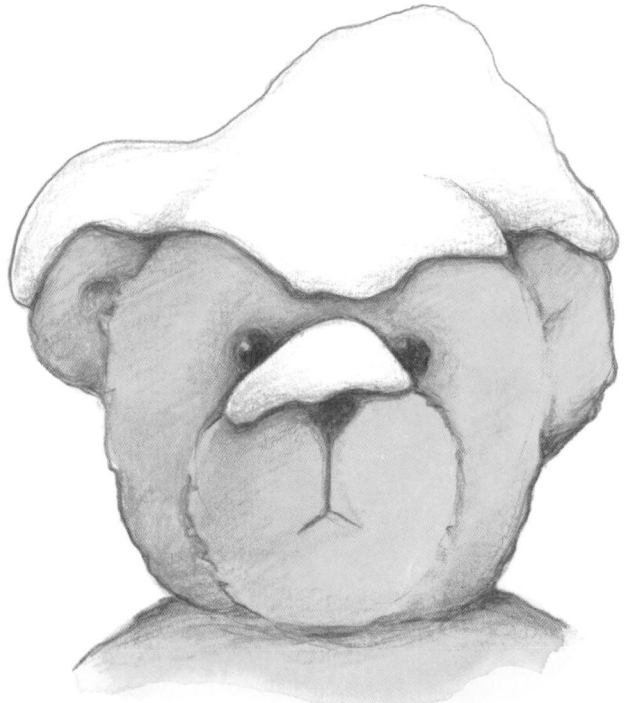

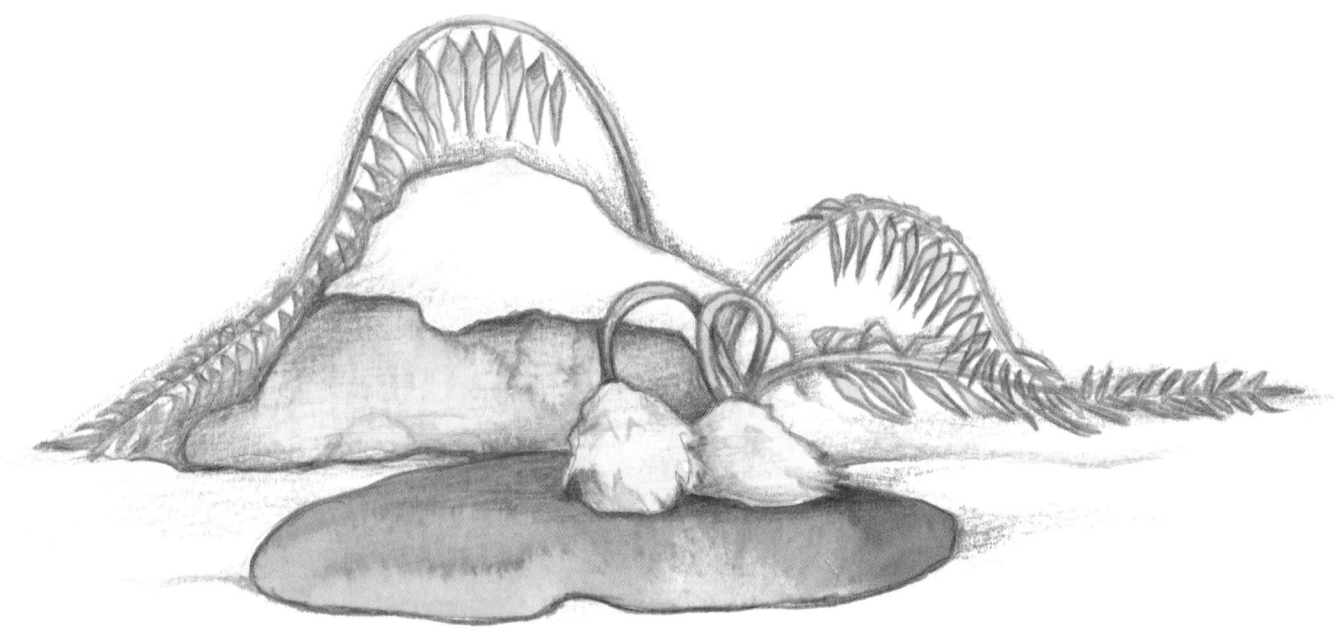

Suddenly noticed, as she felt with her hand,

That when she returned to the house's front stoop,

The plants on her head had all started to droop.

The lilies had wilted and withered away.

The mushrooms were shriveled, their color now gray.

The turtle-shaped moss had plopped to the ground.

The plumes of green fern were now sagging and brown.

There was barely enough for a miniature wreath.

And Ruthie declared through her chattering teeth,

"I do prefer having my old plant-free head,

I'll take care of my hair before I go to bed!"

Back in her house with a dryer in hand,
She dried her wet mane to the very last strand.
She brushed, she combed, and she styled with deft.
Not a single droplet of moisture was left.

But when Ruthie awoke the very next day,
It seemed more trouble was heading her way.
An over-dried scalp plagued Ruthie Bon Bair . . .
Now a flowering cactus poked through her hair!